Read-Along
STORYBOOK AND CD

PLAY TRACK 1 ON YOUR CD NOW!

This is the story of Star Wars: The Phantom Menace. *You can read along with me in your book. You'll know it's time to turn the page when you hear this sound. . . .*

Let's begin now.

Printed in the United States of America

Star Wars: The Phantom Menace Read-Along Storybook and CD First Edition, January 2017

First Bind-Up Edition, March 2019

1 3 5 7 9 10 8 6 4 2

Library of Congress Control Number on file

FAC-029261-19018

ISBN 978-1-368-04350-2

Los Angeles • New York

A LONG TIME AGO IN A GALAXY FAR, FAR AWAY, there was a beautiful planet called Naboo. Although the people of Naboo and their leader, Queen Amidala, were peaceful and kind, the greedy Trade Federation had surrounded the planet with powerful warships. The Trade Federation was using those ships to stop any food or supplies from reaching Naboo.

Two Jedi Knights named Qui-Gon Jinn and Obi-Wan Kenobi traveled to Naboo to help. The Jedi tried to talk to the leaders of the Trade Federation, but the traders attacked them. Deadly droidekas fired as the Jedi drew their lightsabers in defense.

"They have shield generators!"

Qui-Gon knew they had to escape.

"It's a standoff. Let's go!"

The Jedi snuck down to the planet's surface, where they met a friendly alien named Jar Jar Binks. Jar Jar offered to help the Jedi.

"Yousa follow me now, okeyday?"

Jar Jar led them to an underwater city where his people, the Gungans, lived.

Qui-Gon spoke to the Gungan leaders.

"A droid army is about to attack the Naboo. We must warn them."

The Gungans told the Jedi that the fastest way to get to the queen's palace was to travel through the center of the planet. The trip would be very dangerous.

"We'll need a navigator to get us through the planet's core."

Qui-Gon asked if Jar Jar could go with them, and the Gungan leaders agreed.

Qui-Gon, Obi-Wan, and Jar Jar hopped on board a Gungan submarine and began their undersea journey. Suddenly, an eerie blue light began to glow beside them. The light was coming from the giant spikes of a monstrous fish.

Jar Jar did not like that at all.

"Wuh-oh! Big gooberfish!"

The fish grabbed their ship in its razor-sharp teeth and shook it back and forth. There was no escape . . . until a second fish swam up and joined the fight.

"There's always a bigger fish."

Obi-Wan propelled their ship away from the two monsters.

When the trio arrived at the queen's palace, Amidala was already in trouble. Droid soldiers had taken the queen and her guards prisoner.

Qui-Gon and Obi-Wan drew their lightsabers and quickly defeated the battle droids.

Qui-Gon offered to fly the queen to safety.

"If you are to leave, Your Highness, it must be now."

Amidala hated to leave her people. But she knew she needed the Galactic Senate's help to free Naboo. She had to get to Coruscant right away.

The Jedi, Jar Jar, Amidala, and her guards all fled on the queen's personal ship. But the vessel was badly damaged in the escape.

"We'll have to land somewhere to refuel and repair the ship."

They flew to the quiet planet of Tatooine, and Qui-Gon, Jar Jar, and a faithful astromech droid named R2-D2 began

searching for the parts they needed.

The queen had insisted that one of her handmaidens, Padmé, join them, as well.

One junk shop had a working hyperdrive, but Qui-Gon didn't have enough money to pay for it. The owner of the shop, Watto, was very rude to them. But the young boy who worked in the shop was much friendlier.

The boy told them his name was Anakin Skywalker and offered them a place to stay for the night. He even showed Padmé the new droid he was working on!

Anakin introduced the droid as C-3PO.

"Isn't he great? He's not finished yet."

Anakin loved building things. When he wasn't working on C-3PO, he was busy finishing up his new podracer.

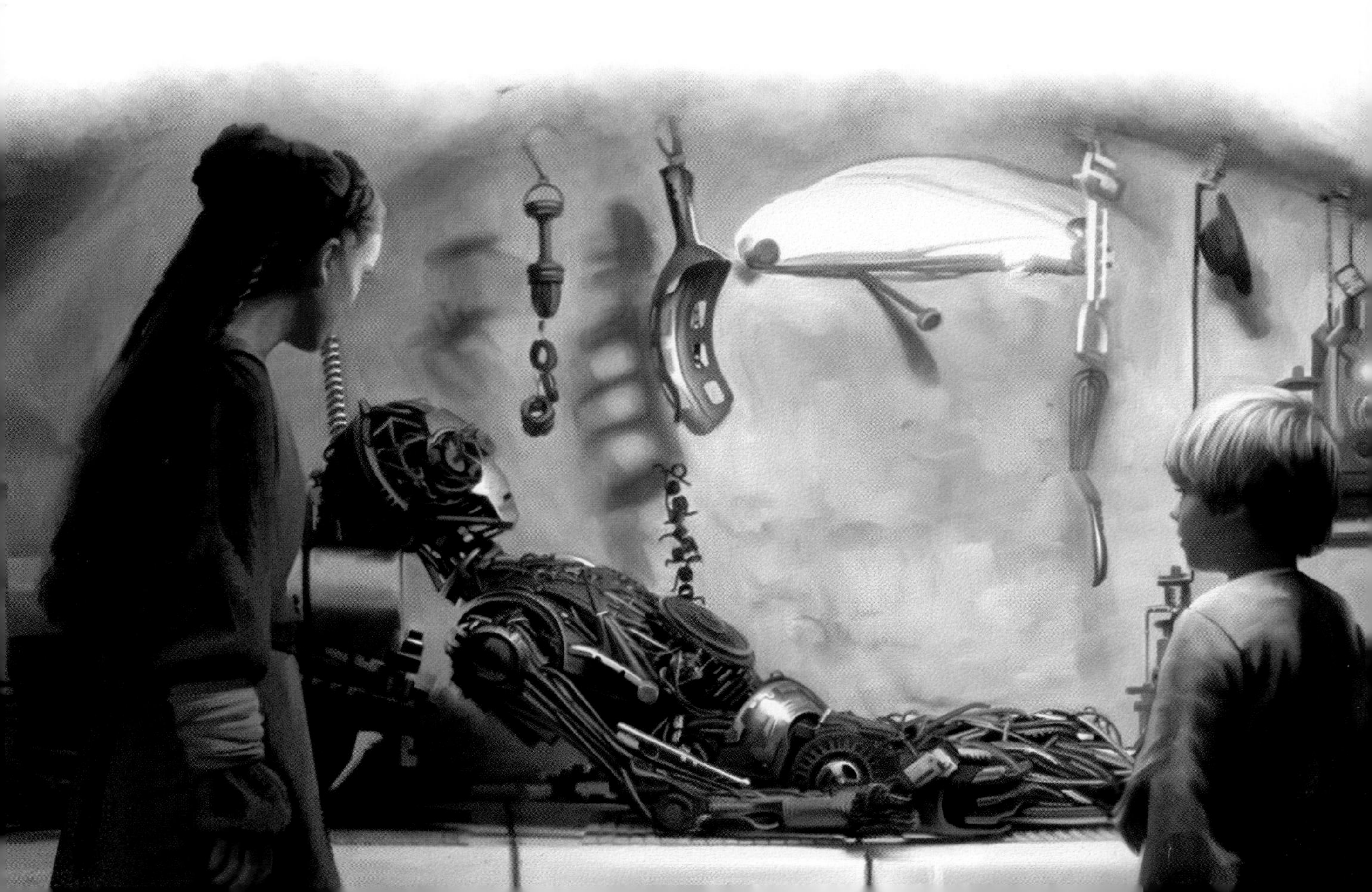

That evening, Anakin's mother, Shmi, served them a delicious meal. They were thankful to the Skywalkers for taking them in, but they were no closer to getting the parts they needed.

Padmé was frustrated.

"These junk dealers must have a weakness of some kind."

That gave Anakin an idea. Watto *did* have a weakness: gambling. If Anakin entered a podrace on their behalf, he could win them the money they needed. It was a risky plan, but Qui-Gon agreed to give it a try.

On the day of the race, Qui-Gon helped Anakin get ready.

"Remember: concentrate on the moment. Use your instincts."

Qui-Gon sensed that the boy had a powerful connection to the Force. The Jedi hoped that if Anakin won the race, he could train him in the ways of the Force.

Qui-Gon's words echoed in Anakin's mind as he focused on each challenge in the race. Even when another podracer pilot tried to destroy Anakin's podracer, Anakin stayed calm.

With the Force guiding him, Anakin won the race!

Now Qui-Gon and his friends could repair their ship. But before he left, Qui-Gon asked Anakin to go with him and become a Jedi. Anakin was excited, but Qui-Gon told him to think through his decision.

"Training to become a Jedi is not an easy challenge. And even if you succeed, it's a hard life."

"But I wanna go. It's what I've always dreamed of doing."

Anakin's mind was made up. He said good-bye to his mother, promising that he would come back someday.

But when Qui-Gon and Anakin reached the ship, someone was waiting for them.

A figure dressed in black ignited a glowing red lightsaber and attacked. Qui-Gon blocked the enemy's blows and told Anakin to run.

"Go! Tell them to take off!"

Qui-Gon's mind raced. Beneath the figure's hood lurked bright yellow eyes, tattooed red skin, and a ring of sharp horns. Who was this monster? And how had it found them on Tatooine?

Obi-Wan saw that his master was in danger and flew the ship closer to the battle. Qui-Gon leapt aboard, leaving the menacing stranger behind.

"What was it?"

"I'm not sure, but it was well trained in the Jedi arts." Qui-Gon shook his head.

"My guess is it was after the queen."

Anakin wanted to help, too.

"What are we gonna do about it?"

But all Qui-Gon would say was that they must be patient. In the meantime, he introduced his students to each other.

"Anakin Skywalker, meet Obi-Wan Kenobi."

When they reached Coruscant, Qui-Gon warned the Jedi Council about the strange figure he had encountered on Tatooine.

"My only conclusion can be that it was a Sith Lord."

The Jedi Council wasn't so sure, except for Jedi Master Yoda.

"Ah, hard to see the dark side is."

Qui-Gon also told them about Anakin. The Jedi Council asked him to bring the boy to them.

Meanwhile, Queen Amidala had some hard decisions to make. The current leader of the Galactic Senate refused to help Naboo. He wanted to investigate the Trade Federation first.

The queen spoke passionately before the Senate.

"I was not elected to watch my people suffer and die while you discuss this invasion in a committee."

She told the Senate it needed a new leader—someone who would take action. Moved by her words, the Senate nominated Senator Palpatine to be its new chancellor. Amidala decided to return to her home planet.

"Captain, ready my ship."

Later on, when the Jedi Council tested Anakin, the members sensed too much fear in him to believe he should be trained as a Jedi.

"Fear is the path to the dark side. Fear leads to anger. Anger leads to hate. Hate leads to suffering."

But Qui-Gon objected.

"I take Anakin as my Padawan learner."

The Council was not convinced. The question of Anakin's training would have to wait. The Jedi were more concerned about protecting the queen on her voyage.

Queen Amidala had a plan. She needed to ask the Gungans for their help in defeating the Trade Federation's army. Once they reached Naboo, Jar Jar led the Jedi, Anakin, Amidala, and her attendants to the Gungans' secret hideout. There, Padmé surprised everyone when she revealed that she was actually Queen Amidala! She pleaded with the Gungan leaders.

"If we do not act quickly, all will be lost forever. I ask you to help us. No, I beg you to help us."

The Gungan leaders agreed to join the fight.

The Trade Federation had already taken over much of Naboo and now prepared for a final battle. But the Trade Federation was not alone in its quest to conquer the planet. It had the aid of a shadowy figure known only as Darth Sidious.

"Wipe them out. All of them."

Even as a hologram, Sidious was terrifying. But his apprentice, Darth Maul, was just as intimidating. It was he who had attacked Qui-Gon on Tatooine. Darth Sidious trusted that Maul could defeat anyone who stood in his way.

The battle soon began. Outside the city, the Trade Federation's droid army passed through the Gungans' protective force fields, but the brave Gungan warriors stood their ground.

Meanwhile, the queen, her guards, and the Jedi snuck into the palace to confront the Trade Federation's leaders.

Qui-Gon sensed the mission would be dangerous, so he told Anakin to hide in a nearby starfighter.

"You'll be safe there."

But the queen and the Jedi did not make it very far into the palace before they met Darth Maul. Qui-Gon turned to Padmé.

“We’ll handle this.”

Maul ignited his two-bladed lightsaber, and Qui-Gon and Obi-Wan leapt into action.

After a long duel throughout the palace, Darth Maul managed to separate the two Jedi, locking Obi-Wan and Qui-Gon behind separate energy fields.

When the barrier between Qui-Gon and Maul vanished, Obi-Wan watched helplessly as Maul attacked Qui-Gon one last time and the Jedi Master fell silently to the ground.

"Nooooooo!"

Obi-Wan broke through the energy barrier and finished the duel his master had begun. Strengthened by the Force, Obi-Wan defeated Maul once and for all.

Anakin had tried to stay put inside his starfighter, but he could tell his friends were in trouble. As he searched for the ship's cannons, he accidentally turned on the autopilot! The starfighter zoomed into space and Anakin joined the battle above Naboo.

Anakin surprised himself with his skill in the cockpit. He dodged enemy fire and managed to blast his way through one of the Trade Federation's warships, destroying it from the inside and disabling the droid army on the planet below!

"Now *this* is podracing!"

The battle was over.

Back at the Jedi Temple, Obi-Wan shared with Yoda how Qui-Gon's last wish was for Obi-Wan to train Anakin in the ways of the Force.

Yoda was unsure.

"Grave danger I fear in his training."

Obi-Wan would not back down.

"I will train Anakin, without the approval of the Council if I must."

Yoda could see there was no changing Obi-Wan's mind, so he agreed.

"Your apprentice, Skywalker will be."

But later Yoda confided in fellow Jedi Master Mace Windu. Yoda could sense great darkness in the Jedi Knights' future, and the defeat of Darth Maul did little to comfort him.

"Always two there are. No more, no less. A master and an apprentice."

And Darth Maul's mysterious master would be a fearsome enemy indeed.

Even though the future was uncertain, there was still much to celebrate. Obi-Wan had earned the title of Jedi Knight and would train Anakin to be the same. Naboo was free, and Queen Amidala could lead her people again. They celebrated side by side with the Gungans, who had fought with them.

For now, the galaxy was at peace.

PLAY TRACK 2 ON YOUR CD NOW!

Read-Along
STORYBOOK AND CD

This is the story of Star Wars: Attack of the Clones. *You can read along with me in your book. You'll know it's time to turn the page when you hear this sound. . . .*

Let's begin now.

Printed in the United States of America

Star Wars: Attack of the Clones Read-Along Storybook and CD First Edition, February 2017

First Bind-Up Edition, March 2019

10 9 8 7 6 5 4 3 2 1

Library of Congress Control Number on file

FAC-029261-19018

ISBN 978-1-368-04350-2

A LONG TIME AGO IN A GALAXY FAR, FAR AWAY, a sleek silver ship flew toward a bustling planet. The ship belonged to Senator Padmé Amidala, former queen of Naboo, and she was on her way to the Galactic Senate on Coruscant.

Many people in the galaxy were unhappy with the Senate. Some, known as the Separatists, even used violence to show how angry they were. Padmé hoped the Senate and the Jedi could bring peace to the galaxy.

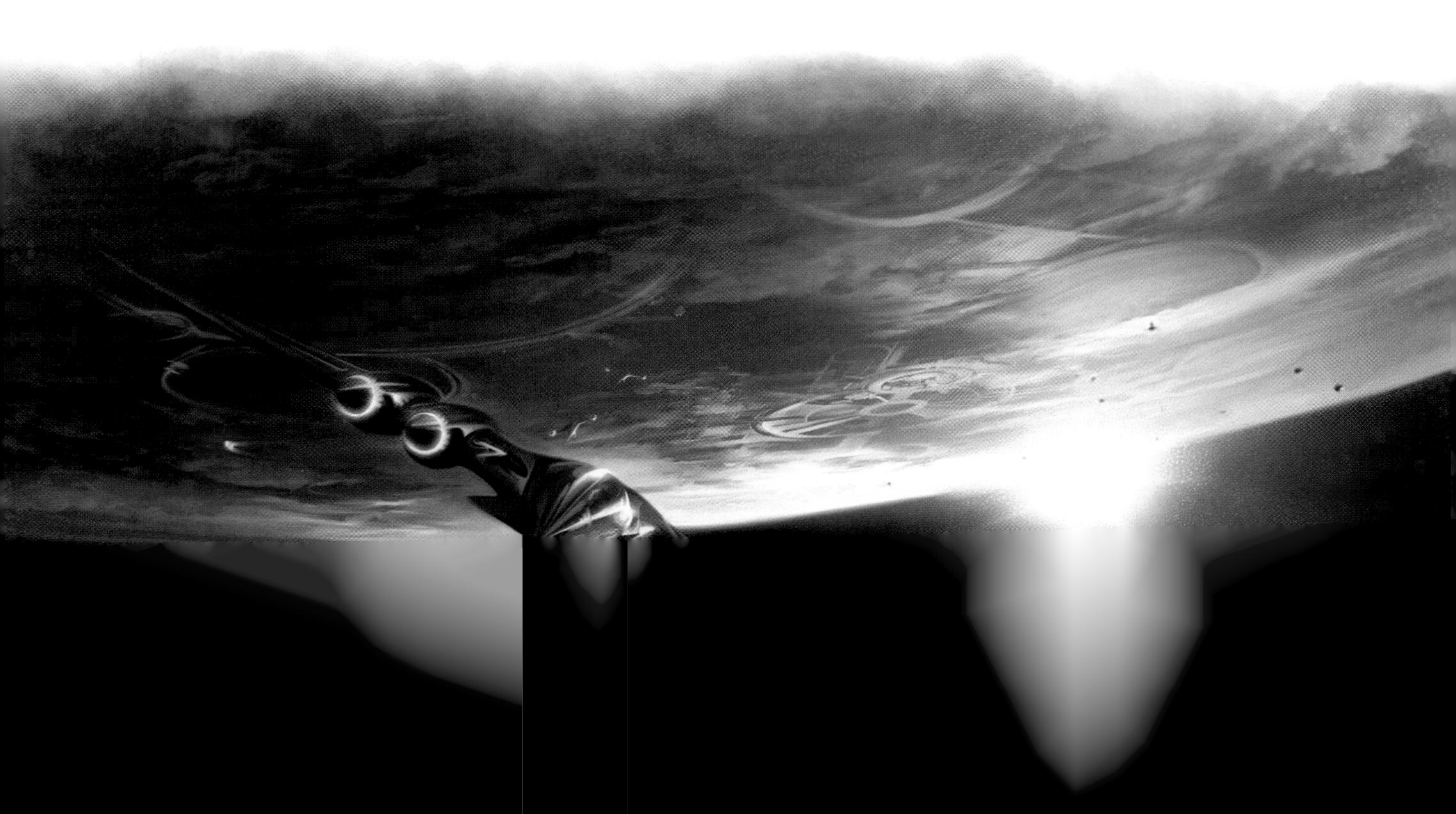

But before Padmé could reach the Senate, there was a huge explosion! Someone had laid a trap for the senator. Padmé escaped the fiery blast, but many of her attendants did not.

"I shouldn't have come back."

Padmé suspected that Count Dooku, the leader of the Separatists, was behind the attack.

Padmé's friends worried that she was still in danger. Even Master Yoda was concerned.

"The dark side clouds everything. Impossible to see, the future is."

Chancellor Palpatine believed that Padmé should be guarded at all times.

"Master Jedi, may I suggest the senator be placed under the protection of your graces?"

Padmé protested, but the Jedi agreed with the Chancellor.

Jedi Knight Obi-Wan Kenobi and his Padawan learner, Anakin Skywalker, arrived to help protect Padmé.

Padmé was excited to see her old friends again.

"It has been far too long, Master Kenobi."

She barely recognized Anakin. It had been ten years since she last saw him. Anakin had thought of Padmé every day since they parted, and he was determined to protect her.

"We will find out who's trying to kill you, Padmé. I promise you."

That night, while Padmé was sleeping, a masked figure released deadly insectoids in her bedroom. Anakin sensed something was wrong and ran to defend Padmé. He and Obi-Wan managed to stop the poisonous creatures, but the mysterious figure fled into the night.

The two Jedi raced after the attacker by speeder, through the bustling city.

"This is a shortcut, I think."

Obi-Wan and Anakin cornered Padmé's attacker in a dark alleyway and questioned her about who had hired her.

"Tell us now!" Anakin could feel his anger getting the better of him.

But before the attacker could answer, a toxic dart silenced her. Anakin and Obi-Wan looked back just in time to glimpse a bounty hunter who had been watching them from the shadows.

It was clear Padmé was no longer safe on Coruscant. She and Anakin left for Naboo while Obi-Wan tried to track down the mysterious bounty hunter.

Padmé turned to Anakin as they boarded the transport. "Suddenly, I'm afraid."

"I am, too." Anakin tried to cheer Padmé up. "Don't worry. We have Artoo with us."

Back at the Jedi Temple, Obi-Wan had discovered that the bounty hunter's dart was from a planet called Kamino.

Obi-Wan went to Yoda for help. He couldn't find the planet's location. The Jedi Master was busy teaching a class of younglings.

"Hmmm, lost a planet, Master Obi-Wan has. How embarrassing. How embarrassing."

Obi-Wan pointed to a map of the galaxy.

"It ought to be here, but it isn't."

One of the younglings determined that someone must have erased the planet from the archives.

Yoda agreed.

"The Padawan is right. Go to the center of gravity's pull and find your planet, you will."

On Naboo, Anakin and Padmé were finally safe. The more time they spent together, the more Padmé and Anakin realized they were falling in love with each other.

But something was still troubling Anakin.

He confessed that he had been having terrible dreams about his mother. He knew that she was in great pain.

"I have to go. I have to help her."

Padmé immediately agreed to journey with Anakin to his home planet of Tatooine.

Meanwhile, Obi-Wan had reached Kamino and discovered a vast army of clones there. An old Jedi Master had hired the Kaminoans to create an army to protect the galaxy. But the Jedi had died before the army was finished, and all knowledge of his plan had been lost.

Obi-Wan reported his findings to the Jedi Council.

"They are using a bounty hunter named Jango Fett to create a clone army. I have a strong feeling that this bounty hunter is the assassin we're looking for."

When Jango Fett learned that Obi-Wan was on Kamino, he tried to escape. Obi-Wan confronted Jango, but the bounty hunter ignited his jet pack and flew out of reach. Then Jango fired a cable around Obi-Wan's hands, forcing him to drop his lightsaber. Obi-Wan used the cable to pull Jango down and kicked him over the side of the landing pad.

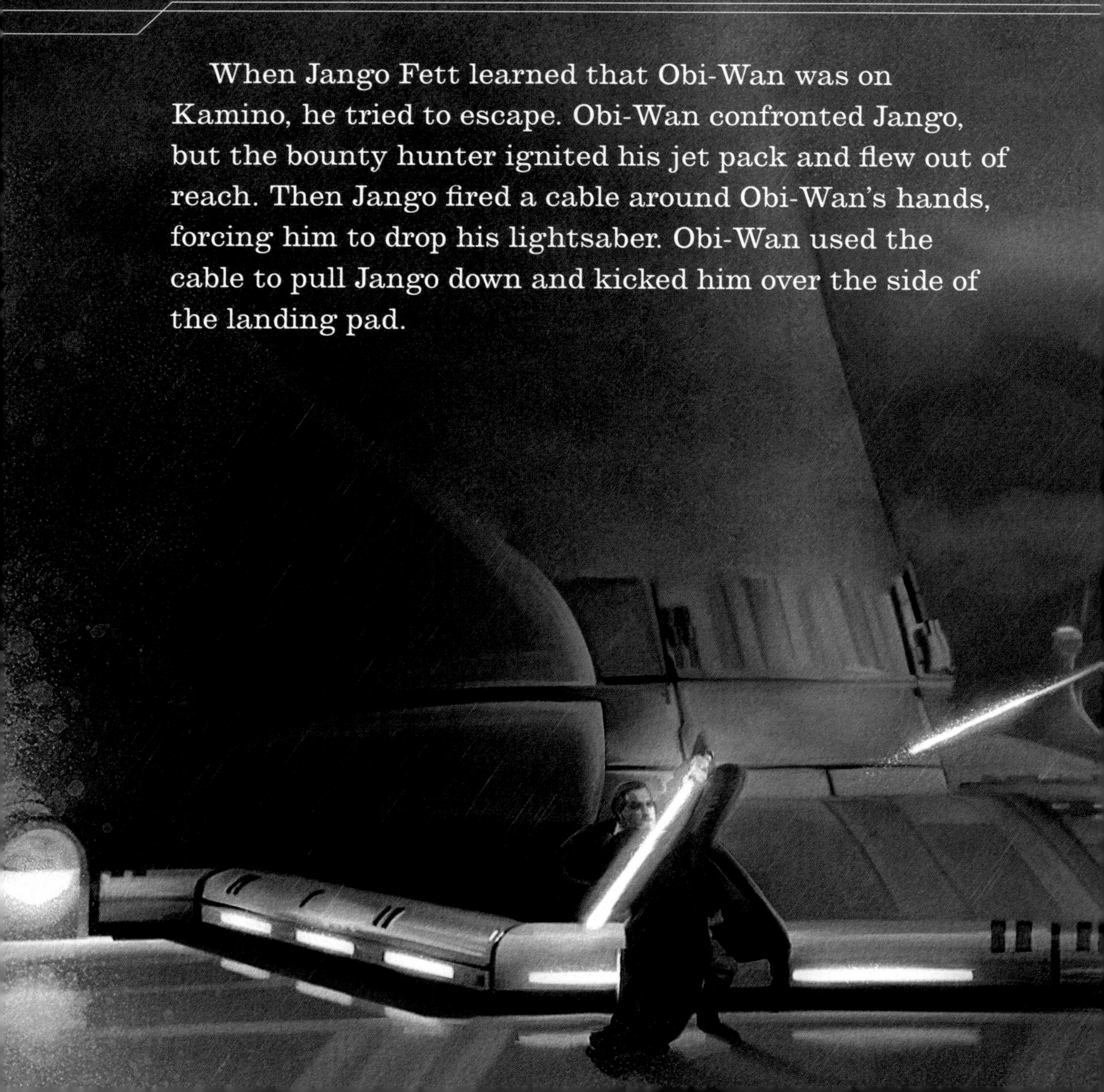

The only problem was Obi-Wan was still tied to the plummeting bounty hunter!

"Oh, not good."

Obi-Wan managed to stop before he fell into the ocean below. But by the time he climbed back up to the landing pad, Jango had escaped in his ship.

While Obi-Wan trailed Jango, Anakin and Padmé searched for Anakin's mother. At her home, they found Anakin's stepfamily and his trusty droid C-3PO. But Anakin's mother was nowhere to be seen. She had been captured by Tusken Raiders.

Anakin told Padmé to wait in safety while he confronted the Tusken Raiders.

"I won't be long."

Obi-Wan had managed to follow Jango all the way to a planet called Geonosis. There, the Separatists were building an army of droids that rivaled Kamino's clone troops.

With two such powerful armies ready to fight, war seemed unavoidable.

"The Jedi will be overwhelmed. The Republic will agree to any demands we make."

Back on Tatooine, Anakin had found his mother, but she was badly hurt.

"I'm here, Mom. You're safe."

Anakin held her tightly. But her wounds were too deep. Anakin felt his mother slip away and become one with the Force.

Hatred filled Anakin's heart. He could never forgive the Tusken Raiders for what they had done. Anakin ignited his lightsaber and attacked the Tusken Raiders' camp.

Far away in the Jedi Temple, Yoda sensed something was not right.

"Something terrible has happened. Young Skywalker is in pain. Terrible pain."

Meanwhile, Obi-Wan tried to warn the Jedi Council of what he had found on Geonosis, but his transmissions were too weak to reach Coruscant.

Instead he reached out to Anakin.

"Anakin? Anakin, do you copy? This is Obi-Wan Kenobi. Anakin?"

Anakin was back with Padmé when he heard Obi-Wan's message. But his master's call for help was cut short when an unseen attacker fired on Obi-Wan. Anakin called the Council, but Padmé knew it was up to her and Anakin to rescue Obi-Wan.

"They'll never get there in time to save him. They have to come halfway across the galaxy."

Obi-Wan had been captured by Count Dooku himself. The Separatist leader tried to convince Obi-Wan that the Senate had been corrupted.

"What if I told you that the Republic was now under the control of the Dark Lord of the Sith?"

"I don't believe you."

"You must join me, Obi-Wan, and together we will destroy the Sith!"

But Obi-Wan refused to listen to Count Dooku.

Anakin and Padmé were unprepared for the enemies who awaited them on Geonosis. After sneaking through the massive droid factory, they were captured by Jango Fett.

As Padmé had suspected, he was working for Count Dooku. The Count threw Anakin, Padmé, and Obi-Wan into a great pit filled with deadly monsters.

Anakin didn't like the look of things.

"I've got a bad feeling about this."

Padmé, Obi-Wan, and Anakin worked together to free themselves from their restraints and bravely fought the vicious creatures Count Dooku had released.

Fortunately, they didn't have to hold off the monsters for long. Soon enough, the Jedi Council arrived to help fight the Separatists.

Mace Windu cornered Count Dooku and demanded his surrender.

Dooku just laughed.

"Brave but foolish, my old Jedi friend. You're impossibly outnumbered."

The Jedi fought valiantly against the droid army. But they were outnumbered.

Count Dooku told Mace Windu to yield.

"Surrender and your lives will be spared."

The situation looked grim.
The Jedi were surrounded.
They couldn't win the battle.

At that moment, the sky filled with Republic transport ships. Yoda had brought the clone army to help. Now the Jedi stood a chance against Dooku.

Yoda took command of the troops.

“Around the survivors, a perimeter create.”

Dooku knew that he had been beaten. The Separatist leader left his droids to hold off the Jedi and headed for his shuttle.

Obi-Wan told Anakin to follow the Count.

"If we catch him, we can end this war right now!"

When the Jedi cornered Dooku, Obi-Wan raised his lightsaber.

"We'll take him together."

But once again, Anakin let his anger get the better of him. He charged at Dooku, slashing wildly at his enemy.

Because Anakin and Obi-Wan weren't working together, the Count quickly defeated both of the young Jedi.

Only one more Jedi stood in Count Dooku's way: Master Yoda. Dooku fired a blast of Force lightning at Yoda.

"I have become more powerful than any Jedi. Even you."

But Yoda simply lifted his hand and absorbed the blast.

"Much to learn you still have."

"It is obvious that this contest cannot be decided by our knowledge of the Force but by our skills with a lightsaber."

The two rivals dueled fiercely until Dooku threatened to crush Anakin and Obi-Wan. Yoda chose to protect his friends, even though it meant letting Dooku escape.

Back on Coruscant, the Jedi made plans for the clone army to join them in the fight against the Separatists.

Obi-Wan addressed Master Yoda.

"I have to admit that without the clones, it would not have been a victory."

"Victory you say?" Yoda shook his head. "Master Obi-Wan, not victory. The shroud of the dark side has fallen. Begun, the Clone War has."

But there was still hope.

Despite the rules of the Jedi Order, Anakin and Padmé secretly wed on Naboo.

Whatever the war was to bring, they would face it together.

PLAY TRACK 3 ON YOUR CD NOW!

Read-Along
STORYBOOK AND CD

This is the story of Star Wars: Revenge of the Sith. *You can read along with me in your book. You'll know it's time to turn the page when you hear this sound. . . .*

Let's begin now.

Printed in the United States of America

Star Wars: Revenge of the Sith Read-Along Storybook and CD First Edition, March 2017

First Bind-Up Edition, March 2019

1 3 5 7 9 10 8 6 4 2

Library of Congress Control Number on file

FAC-029261-19018

ISBN 978-1-368-04350-2

A LONG TIME AGO IN A GALAXY FAR, FAR AWAY, a war was raging. The evil Count Dooku and the commander of his droid army, General Grievous, had attacked the Galactic Senate and kidnapped its leader, Chancellor Palpatine.

Jedi Knights Obi-Wan Kenobi and Anakin Skywalker raced through a swarm of the Count's fighters, toward the ship where the Chancellor was being held captive.

Anakin was confident they would succeed.

"This is where the fun begins."

Count Dooku was waiting for the Jedi on board his ship. Palpatine tried to warn them about the Sith Lord. Obi-Wan simply ignited his lightsaber.

"Chancellor Palpatine, Sith Lords are our specialty."

The Jedi Master dueled with Dooku, but the Count used the Force to trap him beneath a heavy beam. It was up to Anakin to finish the fight and save his friend.

"My powers have doubled since the last time we met, Count."

The young Jedi quickly proved himself and, at Palpatine's urging, defeated Dooku once and for all.

However, General Grievous was not going to let Anakin and Obi-Wan escape with the Chancellor so easily. The evil cyborg was eager to put an end to the Jedi.

"Your lightsabers will make a fine addition to my collection."

Obi-Wan disagreed.

"Not this time. And this time you won't escape."

Anakin and Obi-Wan attacked, forcing Grievous to flee.

When the Jedi returned Palpatine to the Senate on Coruscant, Anakin was able to visit Padmé.

Although marriage was forbidden by the Jedi Order, Anakin and Padmé loved each other deeply and had wed in secret.

That day, Padmé had special news for Anakin.

"Something wonderful has happened."

Anakin and Padmé were going to have a baby.

Meanwhile, Grievous sent word to Darth Sidious about all that had happened. The shadowy figure reassured his loyal servant.

"The end of the war is near, General."

Darth Sidious did not seem concerned by the loss of Dooku.

"Soon I will have a new apprentice. One far younger and more powerful."

Back on Coruscant, Chancellor Palpatine had requested that Anakin act as his personal representative on the Jedi Council. The Council agreed, but Obi-Wan explained the true nature of Anakin's new position later in private.

"The Council wants you to report on all the Chancellor's dealings. They want to know what he's up to."

Anakin did not want to spy on Palpatine. He trusted the Chancellor.

Obi-Wan was not so sure.

"Yes, but use your feelings, Anakin. Something is out of place."

Something was out of place. Anakin had been having terrible nightmares about Padmé. The Jedi believed that death was a natural part of life, but Anakin could not bear the thought of losing her.

The young Jedi shared his fears with Palpatine while they were at the opera. The Chancellor hinted that the dark side of the Force was strong enough to keep people from dying.

That sparked Anakin's curiosity.

"Is it possible to learn this power?"

Palpatine turned to face Anakin.

"Not from a Jedi."

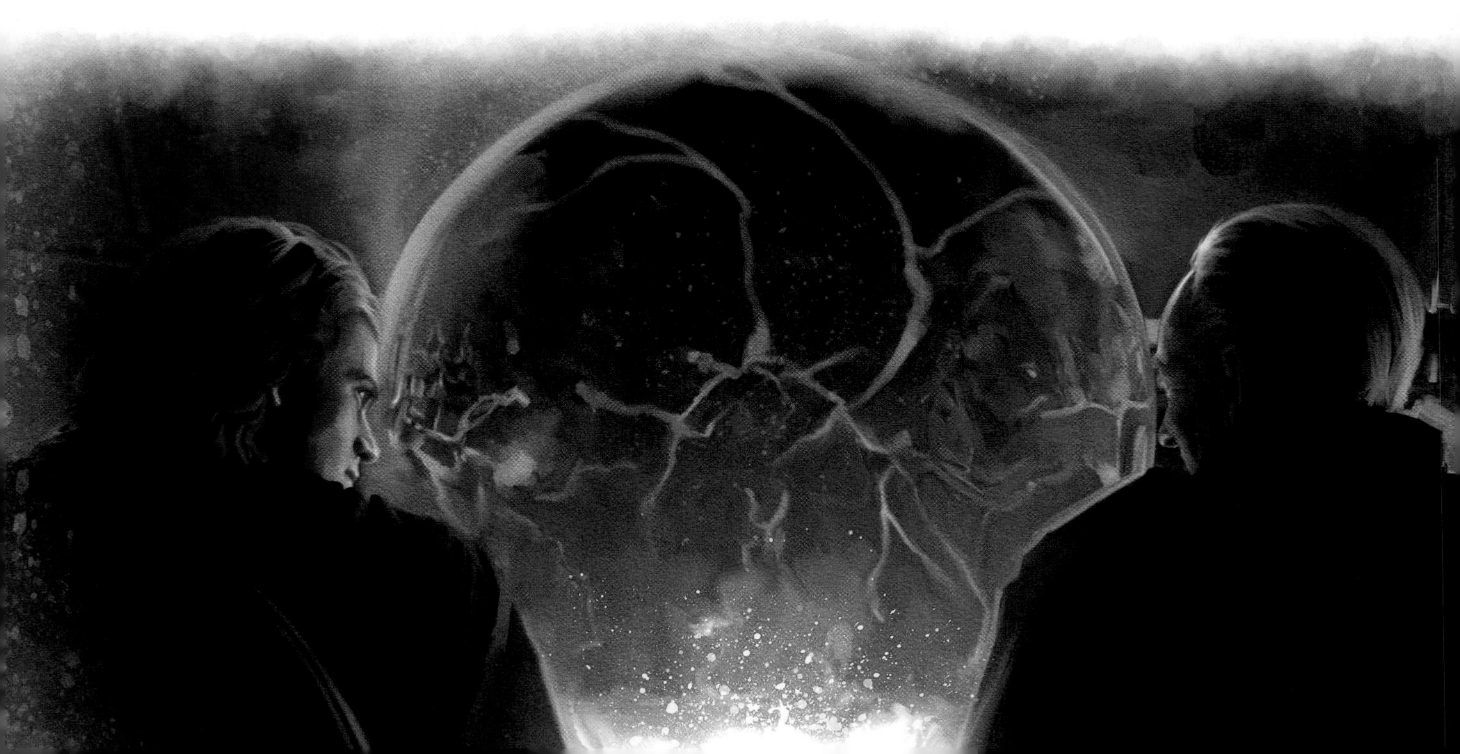

All the while, Obi-Wan was busy tracking down General Grievous. The Jedi Master had followed Grievous to Utapau. There, one of the Pau'an leaders met Obi-Wan and warned him that the general was nearby.

Obi-Wan knew a fight was ahead.

"Tell your people to take shelter."

Obi-Wan soon found the general and his army of droids.
"Hello, there!"
Grievous told his soldiers to stand down.
"Back away! I will deal with this Jedi slime myself."
Obi-Wan ignited his lightsaber.
Grievous ignited four.

"You fool! I have been trained in your Jedi arts by Count Dooku."

Obi-Wan let go of his fear and allowed the Force to guide him.

After a grueling battle, Obi-Wan was finally able to take out Grievous's weapons and put an end to the evil cyborg.

On Coruscant, Palpatine was still urging Anakin to consider the dark side of the Force.

"Only through me can you achieve a power greater than any Jedi. Learn to know the dark side of the Force, and you will be able to save your wife from certain death."

Anakin couldn't believe what he was hearing.

"You're the Sith Lord!"

He finally understood the Jedi Council's concerns.

For years, Palpatine had tricked the Jedi and the Senate by pretending to be their friend. But in reality he was the Sith Lord Darth Sidious. He had been using people on both sides of the war to gain power.

Anakin raced to tell the Council what he had learned. Mace Windu told Anakin to stay behind. He would confront Palpatine with the other Jedi Masters.

Mace Windu was able to hold his own against Palpatine, but the Sith Lord quickly defeated the other Jedi.

Disobeying orders, Anakin arrived just in time to see Mace Windu about to overcome Darth Sidious.

But the evil Sith pleaded with Anakin.

"I have the power to save the one you love."

Anakin gave in to his fear and helped Palpatine defeat Master Windu.

Palpatine was badly scarred in the fight, but he had won a great victory. With his new apprentice, he would be unstoppable.

Anakin was scared.

"I will do whatever you ask. Just help me save Padmé's life."

Darth Sidious reassured Anakin.

"The Force is strong with you. A powerful Sith you will become. Henceforth, you shall be known as Darth Vader."

Darth Sidious had been planning this day for many years. He needed to destroy the Jedi to ensure his total and complete reign.

"Once more, the Sith will rule the galaxy!"

The Sith Lord sent a message to the clone troopers.

"The time has come. Execute Order Sixty-Six."

The clones had been programmed to turn on the Jedi at Darth Sidious's command.

But the clone troopers were not alone.

Anakin himself marched to the Jedi Temple to destroy all he had once held sacred.

Then the young Sith continued on to the volcanic planet of Mustafar.

Yoda and Obi-Wan managed to survive the attack. They snuck back to the Jedi Temple to send out a warning to any other remaining Jedi.

Obi-Wan could hardly believe what had happened.

"Who could have done this?"

He searched the Senate records and found a hologram of Anakin bowing before Palpatine.

Yoda hung his head.

"Twisted by the dark side, young Skywalker has become."

Obi-Wan had to find Anakin, but he did not know where his former Padawan could be. He asked Padmé for help.

"He's in grave danger."

Padmé was worried.

"From the Sith?"

"From himself."

Whatever Anakin was going through, Padmé wouldn't let him face it alone. She knew that Palpatine had sent Anakin on a mission to Mustafar. She decided she would travel there by herself and save him.

Meanwhile, Palpatine had declared himself Emperor. With the Jedi gone, there was no one left to stand in his way . . . or so Palpatine thought.

"I hear a new apprentice you have, Emperor."

Palpatine was shocked to see that Yoda was still alive.

A fierce duel commenced. Yoda and Darth Sidious each used his own side of the Force to try to defeat the other. But the Sith Lord's powers were too strong.

Yoda had no choice but to flee.

Padmé reached Mustafar and found Anakin. But the moment she saw him, she knew something terrible had happened within him. Padmé tried to pull him back from the dark side.

"Stop! Stop now! Come back. I love you."

But Anakin wouldn't listen.

"I'm becoming more powerful than any Jedi has ever dreamed of. And I'm doing it for you. To protect you."

Then Obi-Wan stepped forward from inside Padmé's ship. He had hidden on board to reach Anakin.

Anakin was blinded by his rage.

"You turned her against me!"

"Your anger and your lust for power have already done that."

Obi-Wan realized that nothing could convince Anakin to return to the light. All Anakin felt now was hatred.

"If you're not with me, then you're my enemy."

The two former friends ignited their lightsabers and charged.

Obi-Wan anticipated Anakin's every strike, and Anakin blocked each of Obi-Wan's attacks.

Then Obi-Wan was able to leap up onto a bank, leaving Anakin stranded on a dangerous lava flow.

"It's over, Anakin! I have the high ground."

"You underestimate my power."

Anakin took a running leap but fell short of the bank.

It was the opening Obi-Wan needed. The Jedi Master disarmed Anakin and left him helpless beside the molten river.

Obi-Wan was devastated by all that had happened. He cried out to Anakin, one last time, before leaving him forever.

"You were the chosen one! It was said that you would destroy the Sith, not join them!"

Back on the ship, a heartbroken Padmé doubled over in pain. Obi-Wan rushed her to the med bay, where she gave birth to twins—a boy and a girl she named Luke and Leia.

Padmé spoke of Anakin once more.

"There's good in him. I know. I know there's still . . ."

Then she closed her eyes for the last time.

Obi-Wan, Yoda, and their last remaining ally, Bail Organa, decided to split up Luke and Leia to hide them from Anakin.

Leia would go with Bail to be raised on Alderaan while Obi-Wan took Luke to live with Anakin's family on Tatooine.

Palpatine sensed Anakin's defeat on Mustafar. He retrieved the young Sith from the fiery planet and tended to Anakin's wounds. Anakin had been badly burnt during his duel with Obi-Wan. To keep him alive, Palpatine placed Anakin in protective black armor with a sculpted helmet that altered his voice.

"Lord Vader. Can you hear me?"

"Yes, master."

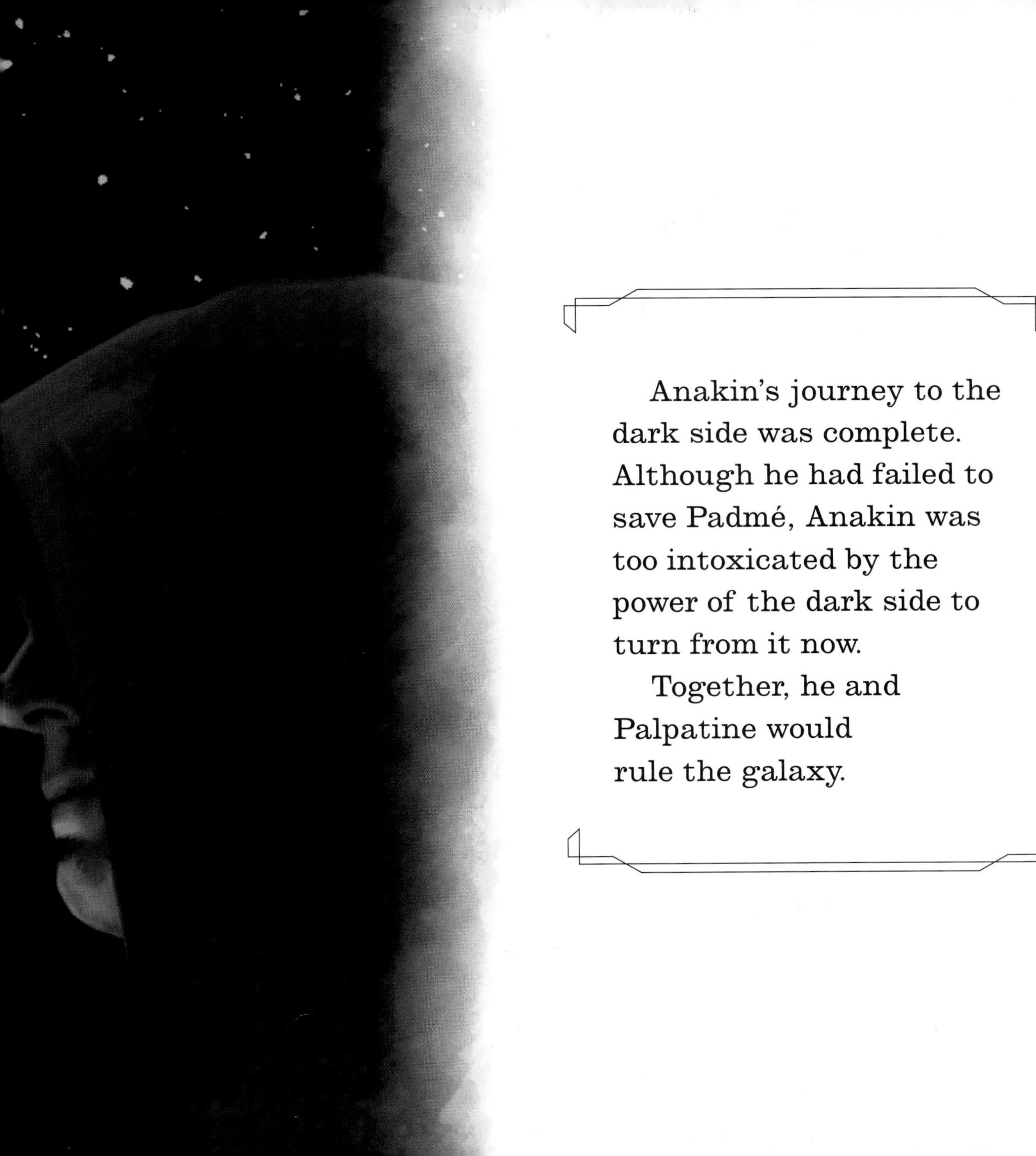

Anakin's journey to the dark side was complete. Although he had failed to save Padmé, Anakin was too intoxicated by the power of the dark side to turn from it now.

Together, he and Palpatine would rule the galaxy.

But far away on the sandy planet of Tatooine, a brighter future was just over the horizon. Obi-Wan had given baby Luke to his uncle Owen and aunt Beru. The young couple smiled down on their new child, unaware that Beru held in her arms the galaxy's last hope.

But that is another story, for another time. . . .